DOWN · BUTTERMILK · LANE

BARBARA MITCHELL

D·O·W·N BUTTERMILK L·A·N·E

JOHN SANDFORD

Lothrop, Lee & Shepard Books   New York

For Sadie and Judy
BM

For my sister
DIANE
Gloria in Excelsis
JS

*The illustrator wishes to thank Kerry and Erin Howard, Dawn
and John McCormick, John and Clara Tate, Pat and Bob Cusek,
Loretta Priola, Susan Pearson, Judit Bodnar, and Marjorie,
Frances and Eleanor Sandford for their patience and
help in the preparation of this book.*

● ● ●

Text copyright © 1993 by Barbara Mitchell
Illustrations copyright © 1993 by John Sandford
*Inquiries should be addressed to Lothrop, Lee & Shepard Books, a
division of William Morrow & Company, Inc., 1350 Avenue of the
Americas, New York, New York 10019. Printed in the
United States of America.*

First Edition 1 2 3 4 5 6 7 8 9 10

*Library of Congress Cataloging in Publication Data
Mitchell, Barbara. Down Buttermilk Lane / by Barbara Mitchell ;
illustrated by John Sandford.
p.   cm.   Summary: An Amish family, traveling by buggy,
spends a day doing errands in the village, visiting, and returning
home in time for supper.
ISBN 0-688-10114-3—ISBN 0-688-10115-1 (lib. bdg.)
[1. Amish—Fiction.   I. Sandford, John, 1948-   ill. II. Title.
PZ7.M686Do   1991   [E]—dc20   90-46876   CIP   AC*

Clip-clip-clip-clip down Buttermilk Lane.
Clop-clop-clop-clop up Horseshoe Road.
Mam and Dat, Rachel, Becky, and Jacob
are off in the buggy.
Rachel and Becky sit in the back.
"Mind now the *blutzes*," says Dat.
The two girls giggle.
They like it when the buggy goes bump.
Jacob sits up front,
right behind Brownie's bobbing tail.
He helps Dat hold the reins
and dreams of having a horse of his own,
just like big brother Ammon.

Clip-clop-clip-clop...
Past fields of rustling cornstalks.
Past black-and-white cows mooing at the morning.
Past farmhouse windows winking at the sun.
Past spinning windmills
and lines of flapping britches.

Up over autumn-brown hills
dotted with barns and silos.
Down by October gardens
striped with cabbages and cauliflowers.

All the way to the village
and Zimmermans general store.
Dat parks the buggy at the hitching rail out front.
The porch is piled high with pumpkins
and baskets of Indian corn.
"Just for nice," says Dat.

Inside is something wonderful!
Giant sacks of oatmeal,
sugar (brown and white),
bags of Gibble's potato chips,
chocolate by the chunk.
The butcher cuts three slices of ring bologna.
"For the *kinder*," he says.
Mam orders a pound of frizzed beef
and a pound of pudding meat.
"For Dawdi…a present, yes."

Dat and Jacob go upstairs.
Dat needs socks and suspenders.
Jacob tries on winter hats.

Mam and Rachel and Becky
go down the street to Zooks Dry Goods.
Rachel reads off the names of quilt patterns:
"Shoofly, Windmill Blades, Sunshine and Shadow,
Broken Star."
"The Star for our Lyddie, I think," says Mam.
On snowy winter afternoons,
Mam and Mammi and the aunts
will sew on Lyddie's wedding quilt.

Then clip-clop-clip-clop
down the road to Bird-in-Hand.
Dat must stop at the hardware.
Jacob and Rachel rush to the checkerboard
that sits on a barrel by the stove.
Ach!
They must wait their turn.
Gents who live in the village
are having their morning game.

Mam and Becky walk over to the Farmers Market
to say hello to Cousin Hazel.
Hazel sells pies to the *English*.
"Such a crowd it is today!" she says.
Hazel has been there since sunrise,
selling pumpkin, vanilla, and shoofly pies
baked at midnight "for fresh."
The pies make Becky's mouth water.
"It makes time for dinner," says Mam.

Clip-clop-clip-clop
down the road to Dawdi's place.
Mammi has dinner all set out:
chicken potpie with noodles,
green beans with ham,
slaw and red beet eggs,
a loaf of home-baked bread,
and a pitcher of cold apple cider.
"Apple dumplings for sweet," says Dawdi.
But Jacob and Rachel and Becky
have already eaten themselves full.
They must take their dumplings home in a sack.

After dinner
Dat and Dawdi and the children
stroll down to the pond.
The ducks swim round and round
in the lazy autumn afternoon.
"It makes time for milking,"
Dat says at last.

Brownie balks.
He does not like to start out on hills.
Soon off they go again,
clip-clop-clip-clop…

Past Ebersol Chair Shop,
where the chair maker sets out rockers
bright with flowers and acorns.

"Listen yet," says Mam.
Over by Fishers Carriage Shop
a walnut tree is dropping its heavy fruit,
plop, plop-plop, plop.
Dat stops the buggy to listen.
"Ya," the buggy maker says,
"it gives wonderful this year.
Take for yourselves a bunch."

Becky sits up front now,
her head against Mam's arm,
as Dat drives slowly
clip...clop...clip...clop
down Horseshoe Road,
up Buttermilk Lane,
home to the big white farmhouse.

Home to sleepy-eyed mules
eager to be fed.

Home to lined-up cows
impatient to be milked.

Home, to the warm farmhouse kitchen
and Mammi's dumplings for supper.

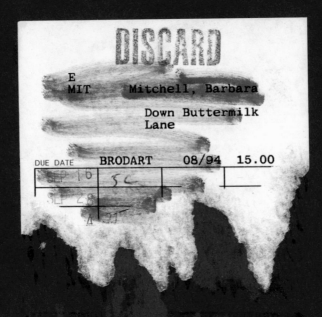